CHOMPER

My Bearded Dragon

Keep smiling!

Written by: **Carmen Swick**

Illustrated by: **Joey Manfre**

For information on "Chomper my Bearded Dragon"
www.carmenswick.com email: carmens222@gmail.com

The Author of this book is not a herpetologist. The intent of the author is to share this adventurous, fictional story for your reading enjoyment.

Carmen Swick's Editor: Page Lambert

Illustrator: Joey Manfre

Cover design: Joey Manfre

PRESBEAU
PUBLISHING

Publisher: Presbeau Publishing Inc.

ISBN# 978-0-9831380-6-8

Library of Congress Control #2015946432

Printed and Bound and Published in the United States of America.

Chomper my Bearded Dragon: www.carmenswick.com

Other books by this Author: Patch land Adventures Series, and Coloring book & activity sheets.

Cast of Characters

CHOMPER
A Bearded Dragon from Colorado

BENNY
Chomper's Human Friend

BANROO
A Mischevious Kangaroo

MR. KOALA
A Wise Koala

UNCLE HERMAN
Chomper's Uncle who lives in Australia

DEDICATION

I am dedicating this page to everyone, to every animal and creature
that has been impacted by the tragic fires in Australia. I am saddened
to hear of the devastation that has been left behind far and wide.
It has been the worst wildfires seen in decades.

Thank you to the rescue-firefighters, and to the many humanitarians
and donors during these times, as every effort has not gone unseen.
May your beautiful country and eco system regrow and flourish.

May peace and love be with you good folks in Australia.

- Carmen Swick

Hi, my name is Chomper. I am a female bearded dragon. I live in Colorado with my human brother Benny and his family.

I would like to meet my lizard family that lives in Australia! Did you know that's where the bearded dragons come from?

Maybe Benny would like to go.
We can take one of Uncle Geno's planes!

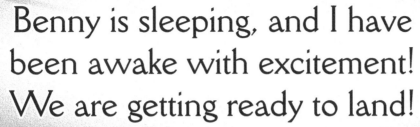

Benny is sleeping, and I have been awake with excitement! We are getting ready to land!

Finally, we are here. Benny and I have the map to go look for my family! Uncle Geno will meet us back at the hotel before dark.

Benny, my map says to go in this direction.
Hey! That Kangaroo just stole my map!
Now we will never find my family.

Chomper, don't cry. We will find
the Kangaroo with the map. We
will ask the other animals if they
know who this mischievous
Kangaroo is.

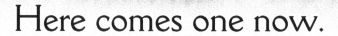
Here comes one now.
Hi Mr. Koala, have you seen a Kangaroo with a map? She snatched it from my buddy Chomper.

Herman? I know him. He wears glasses and a fedora hat. I am sorry, I wasn't trying to make you sad. I was just having a little fun. I can take you there. You can ride in my pouch. That's how Kangaroo mommies carry their babies. Your friend can ride on my back.

Okay Banroo. Stop being so mischievous!

Here we are.
That's Uncle Herman on the hammock, and he is wearing glasses and a fedora hat.

Also, be careful while walking around. Australia is known for having the most amazing wildlife, and dangerous species of snakes, spiders, bees, and the stinging stonefish that are found in Australia's reefs.

Uncle Herman, we will, and we would like to meet you at the beach tomorrow. Banroo is taking us back to the hotel before it gets dark. See you in the morning.

Look! There is a dingo dog!
They are native to Australia.

Good day, Chomper. I would like to show you the Biscuit Starfish that is native to Australia. The colors are a glowing red and orange. You can discover them in the shallow waters of the ocean floor.

Here we are! Hi, Uncle Herman.

I love the colors!

I will make a starfish in the sand and then we need to head back to the hotel since we are leaving in the morning. This was a quick trip for us, so we could meet you.

Chomper, I would like to
give you my fedora hat.

Wow! Thank you. Goodbye!

Benny, thank you for the greatest experience!

Comprehension/study guide.

1.) Where does Chomper live?

2.) Where do bearded dragons come from?

3.) Whose plane did they take to Australia?

4.) Does Uncle Herman wear glasses?

5.) Who took the map?

6.) Can you name some of the
   dangerous animals in Australia?

7.) What color is the Biscuit Starfish?

About the Author:

I live in Colorado with my family and enjoy the outdoor activities that the Centennial state has to offer. I am a member for the Society of Children's Book Writers and Illustrators. I volunteered for a non-profit organization, The Foundation Fighting Blindness, where I held the position as the President of the Denver Chapter, for the past 11 years. I was the Chair for The Blind Taste of the Rockies, which is an annual fundraiser to raise awareness, and funds to help find a cure for blindness. In 2012 I led the role of Chair for the Denver Vision walk. In 2018 and 2019 I was the Chair for the Ride for Sight "poker run" fundraiser, all the while attending schools and libraries, for presentations/workshops and signings for the Patch land Adventure series. I also was the presenting children's book author for the 2014 Young Writers Conference for Jeffco Elementary Schools.

About the Illustrator:

Joey Manfre is a graphic designer/illustrator living in Northern California. Professionally, he has worked on projects ranging from fancy wine packaging to funky tee shirts. He has a special fondness for illustrating books, especially whimsical stories of adventure. When not creating visually, he enjoys quality time with his lovely wife Jan and their pupdog Won Ton...but his sketchbook is always close at hand. Examples of his works can be seen at www.joeymanfredesign.com.

CPSIA information can be obtained
at www.ICGtesting.com
Printed in the USA
BVHW021742130621
609475BV00018B/790

9 780983 138068